Zarua D. Maning

The Witch's Prophecy

The Witch's Prophecy

By

Zarua D. Maning

Love, magic, and destiny awaits.

Dedication

To my sister witches and lovers of the paranormal around the world,

From the depths of our shared magic, I offer this tale. As the moon guides the tides, may our bonds strengthen through every challenge and triumph we face. Together, we dance under the starlit sky, casting spells that weave our destinies. This story is for you, who embrace the shadows and the light, who find beauty in the unknown and power in the mystical. May "The Witch's Prophecy" ignite your spirit and remind you that we are never alone in our journey.

Blessed be,

Zarua D. Maning

Prologue

The night was alive with whispers, the forest cloaked in shadows that danced beneath the pale moonlight. Ancient trees stood as silent sentinels, their gnarled branches stretching towards the heavens like skeletal fingers. In the heart of this enchanted forest, where time seemed to hold its breath, a powerful ritual was underway.

Celeste Darkmoon stood at the center of a circle of seven witches, her raven-black hair cascading over her shoulders like a dark waterfall. Her emerald eyes glowed with an inner light, reflecting the strength and resolve that flowed through her veins. Around her, the coven chanted in unison, their voices rising and falling like the tides of an otherworldly sea.

A cauldron bubbled with a mixture of rare herbs and enchanted ingredients, its fumes filling the air with a heady, intoxicating scent. The ground beneath them pulsed with energy, the very earth responding to their call. They were preparing for a journey through time, a quest to rewrite the past and safeguard the future.

Celeste's heart pounded with anticipation and fear. She had seen the vision—Gabriel, the vampire with piercing blue eyes and a soul weighed down by centuries of darkness, would soon face a fate worse than death. The hunters, relentless in their pursuit, would not stop until they had extinguished his life. She could not let that happen.

As she chanted the ancient incantation, Celeste felt a surge of power unlike anything she had ever known. The portal shimmered into existence, a golden gateway that bridged the present and the past. Her coven's magic, combined with Gabriel's vampiric essence, had created a conduit through time itself.

Gabriel stepped into the circle, his presence commanding and enigmatic. He had lived for centuries, a solitary figure navigating a world that feared and hunted his kind. Yet, in Celeste's eyes, he found something he had thought lost forever—hope. Together, they would face the unknown, their fates intertwined by the threads of destiny.

"Are you ready?" Celeste asked, her voice steady despite the storm of emotions within her.

Gabriel nodded; his expression resolute. "With you, I am ready for anything."

Hand in hand, they stepped through the portal, their surroundings blurring and shifting as they embarked on their perilous journey. The forest around them faded away, replaced by a landscape of unfamiliar sights and sounds. They had crossed the threshold into a time long past, where their actions would shape the course of history.

But the path ahead was fraught with danger. The hunters were not their only adversaries; dark forces lurked in the shadows, waiting for the moment to strike. Celeste knew that their mission would test the limits of their strength and courage, but she was determined to see it through.

For within her chest burned a fire of defiance and love, a beacon that would guide them through the darkest of nights. And as the first light of dawn began to break on the horizon, Celeste whispered a silent vow—to protect Gabriel, to fight for their future, and to embrace whatever fate had in store.

The journey had begun, and there was no turning back.

Zarua D. Maning

Table of Contents

The Witch's Prophecy

Chapter 1
The Witch's Vision

Celeste Darkmoon woke to the soft glow of dawn filtering through her bedroom window. The air was filled with the scent of lavender and sage, remnants from the night's rituals. Her quaint little shop, "Darkmoon Mystics," sat in the heart of a town that seemed to have one foot in the present and another in an enchanted past. The cobblestone streets, lined with old-fashioned lampposts and quaint shops, added to the town's magical charm. As she prepared for the day, she couldn't shake the feeling that something extraordinary was about to happen.

Her day began as it always did, with a steaming cup of herbal tea and the gentle hum of her cat, Shadow, who seemed to sense the magic in the air. Celeste's shop was a sanctuary for those seeking guidance and solace. Shelves lined with ancient tomes and mystical artifacts created an atmosphere that was both inviting and mysterious. The centerpiece of the room was her tarot reading table, adorned with a deep purple cloth and an array of crystals.

As the clock struck nine, the bell above the door chimed softly, announcing the arrival of her first client. Celeste greeted them with a warm smile, her emerald eyes sparkling with kindness. She settled into the familiar routine, letting the cards guide her words and provide comfort to those who sought her wisdom.

Mid-morning, the shop door opened, and a figure stepped in, instantly capturing Celeste's attention. He was strikingly handsome, with blond hair that caught the light and piercing blue eyes that seemed to see right through her. His presence was almost otherworldly, and Celeste felt a shiver of recognition. This man was no ordinary client.

"Good morning," she greeted, her voice steady despite the flutter in her chest. "How can I help you today?"

"I've heard about your readings," he said, his voice smooth and melodic. "They say you're the best."

Celeste motioned for him to sit at her table. As she shuffled the tarot deck, she sensed a powerful energy emanating from him. She laid out the cards, each one revealing more about the man before her. The final card made her heart stop – The Tower, a symbol of sudden change and upheaval.

A vision flooded her mind: Gabriel, the vampire, surrounded by darkness, his body lifeless, and a group of hunters closing in. The vividness of the vision left her breathless. She knew she had to warn him.

"Who are you?" she asked, her voice barely above a whisper.

"My name is Gabriel," he replied, his eyes locking onto hers. "And I believe you've seen something I need to know."

Celeste took a deep breath, steadying herself. "You're in grave danger, Gabriel. I saw a group of hunters. They're planning to kill you."

Gabriel's expression remained calm, but a flicker of fear crossed his eyes. "I've been running from them for centuries. Why now?"

"I don't know," Celeste admitted. "But the vision was clear. They will find you soon unless we do something."

Celeste's mind raced. She knew she couldn't let Gabriel face this alone. "I can help you," she said, determination in her voice. "My coven and I have the power to protect you. We need to act quickly."

Gabriel looked at her, a mixture of hope and skepticism in his eyes. "Why would you help me? I'm a vampire. Most people fear us."

"I've never been one to follow the crowd," Celeste replied with a wry smile. "Besides, I believe our fates are intertwined. There's a reason you came to me."

Over the next few days, Celeste and Gabriel spent every moment together, planning their next move. Celeste introduced him to her coven, seven powerful witches each with unique abilities. Together, they began researching ways to prevent the hunters from ever becoming a threat.

As they worked side by side, a bond formed between Celeste and Gabriel. They shared stories of their pasts, their hopes, and their fears. The more time they spent together, the stronger their connection grew. It wasn't long before their friendship began to blossom into something more profound, a love that neither had expected but both desperately needed.

The coven's plan was daring: to combine their magic with Gabriel's vampiric abilities to travel back in time and stop the hunters before they could even start. It was a risky endeavor, but they were willing to take the chance to save Gabriel and protect their future.

Chapter 2
<u>Unveiling Secrets</u>

Gabriel's story began centuries ago in a small village nestled deep in the Carpathian Mountains. He was born into a noble family, revered for their wealth and influence. However, his life took a dark turn when he was turned into a vampire by an ancient, malevolent force. The transformation left him with heightened senses, extraordinary strength, and an insatiable thirst for blood. Despite the darkness within him, Gabriel retained a glimmer of humanity, a desire to protect the innocent and seek redemption for his cursed existence.

As he shared his story with Celeste, she listened intently, her heart aching for the pain and loneliness he had endured. Gabriel spoke of his countless battles with vampire hunters, each encounter more harrowing than the last. The hunters were relentless, driven by a deep-seated hatred for his kind. Gabriel had lost friends and allies over the years, but he had always managed to stay one step ahead – until now.

Celeste introduced Gabriel to her coven, a diverse group of seven witches each possessing unique abilities. There was Ravenna, the fiery redhead with a talent for elemental magic; Lyra, the serene and wise healer; Thalia, the mischievous illusionist; Nyx, the dark and mysterious necromancer; Cassia, the knowledgeable alchemist; Iris, the empath with the power to sense and manipulate emotions; and Rowan, the fierce and loyal warrior.

The coven welcomed Gabriel with open arms, recognizing the urgency of their mission. Together, they devised a plan to use their combined magical abilities to protect him from the hunters. Each witch brought their own strengths to the table, creating a powerful synergy that would be crucial in the battles to come.

The vampire hunters were a formidable force, led by a man named Alaric. He was a seasoned warrior, scarred from years of hunting vampires. His hatred for them was personal – his family had been slaughtered by vampires when he was just a boy. Alaric's vendetta drove him to assemble a team of elite hunters, each with their own tragic stories and reasons for joining the cause.

The hunters operated in the shadows, using advanced weaponry and ancient techniques passed down through generations. Their base was hidden in a remote location, fortified with traps and wards to keep vampires at bay. Alaric's obsession with eradicating vampires blinded him to the possibility of coexistence, fueling his determination to kill Gabriel at any cost.

In the heart of Celeste's shop, the coven and Gabriel gathered around a large wooden table, maps and magical artifacts spread out before them. They knew the hunters would strike soon, and they had to be prepared. Celeste used her scrying crystal to locate the hunters' base, revealing its hidden location in a dense forest.

"We need to strike first," Celeste said, her voice filled with resolve. "If we can take out their leader, the rest will scatter."

Gabriel nodded, his eyes reflecting the same determination. "I agree. But we need to be careful. Alaric is cunning and ruthless. We can't underestimate him."

The coven worked tirelessly, crafting protective charms and defensive spells. They practiced their magic, honing their skills for the imminent battle. Gabriel shared his knowledge of the hunters' tactics, helping them anticipate their moves and counter their strategies.

As the sun set, casting a golden glow over the town, the coven made their final preparations. Celeste led them in a ritual, invoking the protection of the ancient spirits and drawing upon the power of the earth. The air crackled with energy, and a sense of unity and purpose filled the room.

Gabriel stood at the edge of the circle, feeling a sense of belonging he hadn't felt in centuries. These witches were more than allies – they were friends, bound by a common goal. He looked at Celeste, her face illuminated by the flickering candlelight, and felt a surge of gratitude. She had given him hope, and for the first time in a long while, he believed they might succeed.

The stage was set for an epic confrontation. The coven was ready, their magic strong and their spirits unyielding. They knew the path ahead would be fraught with danger, but they were prepared to face it together. The bond between Celeste and Gabriel grew stronger with each passing moment, setting the stage for a love story intertwined with magic, danger, and destiny.

Chapter 3
Time-Traveling Magic

Under the twilight sky, Celeste and her coven prepared for the most complex ritual they had ever attempted. The air was thick with the scent of burning sage and the soft hum of ancient incantations. Gabriel stood at the center of the circle, feeling the energy swirl around him. The witches formed a ring, their hands linked, each one channeling their unique power into the spell.

Celeste's voice rose above the others, clear and commanding. "Spirits of time and space, hear our call. Bend the fabric of reality and allow us passage to the past. Guide us to the moment before the hunters' path began."

The ground beneath them trembled as the magic took hold. A shimmering portal began to form, its edges glowing with a golden light. The coven's combined power, amplified by Gabriel's vampiric essence, created a bridge between times. With a final, powerful incantation, the portal stabilized, and the group stepped through, their surroundings blurring and shifting as they traveled back in time.

The world around them transformed, colors and shapes melting and reforming into a new landscape. They found themselves in a dense forest, the air filled with the scent of pine and damp earth. The sound of birdsong and rustling leaves replaced the modern hum of machinery. It was a simpler, yet more dangerous time.

Celeste took a deep breath, grounding herself in this new reality. "We've made it," she said, her voice tinged with awe and relief. "But we must be cautious. We don't know what dangers await us here."

Gabriel nodded, his senses on high alert. "We need to find the village where Alaric's family was attacked. If we can prevent that event, we might change the course of his life and stop the formation of the hunters."

They moved silently through the forest, their footsteps barely making a sound on the moss-covered ground. Each member of the coven used their abilities to navigate and protect the group. Seraphina controlled the elements to clear their path, while Lyra's healing magic kept them energized and focused.

As they traveled, they encountered various historical figures and landmarks. They saw villages and towns in their early stages, met with local healers and wise women who recognized Celeste's power and offered their aid. The group forged alliances, gathered information, and learned about the customs and dangers of this ancient time.

One evening, they found themselves at a bustling marketplace. The air was filled with the smell of fresh bread, herbs, and the smoky scent of roasting meat. The sounds of merchants hawking their wares and children playing filled the air, a stark contrast to the impending danger they faced.

Celeste and Gabriel wandered through the market, marveling at the simplicity and vibrancy of the life around them.

Despite the gravity of their mission, they couldn't help but enjoy these moments of normalcy and connection. It was in these quiet moments that their bond deepened, their conversations flowing easily as they shared their thoughts and dreams.

As days turned into weeks, the connection between Celeste and Gabriel grew stronger. They found themselves drawn to each other, not just by the urgency of their mission but by a deeper, more personal bond. They spent evenings talking by the fire, sharing stories of their past and hopes for the future.

One night, as they sat under the starlit sky, Gabriel took Celeste's hand. "You've given me something I thought I'd lost forever," he said, his voice soft. "Hope. For the first time in centuries, I feel like there's a future worth fighting for."

Celeste looked into his eyes, feeling the truth of his words resonate within her. "We're in this together, Gabriel. Whatever happens, we face it as one."

Their friendship blossomed into a love that transcended time and magic, a bond that gave them the strength to face the challenges ahead. The coven noticed the change, their unity and determination growing stronger with each passing day.

The peace and camaraderie were shattered one night when the hunters ambushed them. The attack was sudden and brutal, the quiet of the night exploding into chaos. Alaric and his team had found them, and they showed no mercy.

Celeste and her coven fought back with all their might. Seraphina unleashed a torrent of fire, while Nyx summoned spirits to aid them. Gabriel's vampiric strength and speed made him a formidable opponent, his movements a blur as he fought off the attackers.

Despite their combined power, the hunters were relentless. The battle raged on, the forest echoing with the sounds of magic and combat. Celeste found herself face-to-face with Alaric, their eyes locking in a moment of understanding and hatred.

"You can't stop us," Alaric hissed, his blade glinting in the moonlight. "We will rid the world of your kind."

Celeste's resolve hardened. "Not if we stop you first," she replied, channeling her magic into a powerful blast that knocked him back.

The hunters retreated, but the message was clear: the fight was far from over. The coven regrouped; their determination stronger than ever. They knew they had to act quickly, to find the moment that set Alaric on his path of vengeance and change it forever.

The stakes were higher than ever, and the bond between Celeste and Gabriel was the key to their success. Together, they would face whatever challenges lay ahead, their love and magic intertwined in a battle against time itself.

Chapter 4
<u>Battling the Hunters</u>

With the immediate threat of the hunters pushed back, Celeste and her coven regrouped to strategize. The atmosphere was tense, the air thick with the smell of burnt wood and magic residue. They gathered around a large map of the region, marking key locations and potential points of attack.

Celeste traced her finger along a path leading to a small village nestled in a valley. "This is where Alaric's family was attacked," she said, her voice firm. "We need to prevent that event. If we can save his family, we might alter his course."

Gabriel nodded, his eyes fixed on the map. "It won't be easy. The hunters will be expecting us, and we'll need to be careful not to disrupt the timeline too much."

The coven members voiced their agreement, each suggesting ways they could use their abilities to achieve their goal. Seraphina proposed using her elemental magic to create diversions, while Lyra suggested casting protective spells around the village.

The next day, the group set out towards the village. The journey was arduous, the terrain rough and unforgiving. As they approached, Celeste sensed a shift in the air – a sign that the hunters were already nearby.

The village was quiet, its inhabitants unaware of the impending danger. Celeste and her coven spread out, each taking a position to defend the village. Seraphina summoned a storm, dark clouds gathering overhead, while Nyx called upon spirits to watch over them.

The first attack came at dusk. Hunters emerged from the shadows, their weapons gleaming in the fading light. Celeste stood her ground, her magic crackling around her. She cast a spell of protection over the village, a shimmering barrier that would repel the hunters.

The battle was fierce, spells and weapons clashing in a deadly dance. Celeste's heart pounded as she faced off against a group of hunters, her magic weaving a shield around her. She could feel the strain, but her determination never wavered.

Gabriel fought alongside the witches, his vampiric abilities giving him an edge in the battle. He moved with supernatural speed, his attacks precise and deadly. He felt a surge of protectiveness for the witches, especially Celeste, whose courage and strength inspired him.

In the heat of the battle, Gabriel found himself facing Alaric. The hunter's eyes burned with hatred; his blade aimed at Gabriel's heart. "You cannot win," Alaric snarled, lunging forward.

Gabriel parried the attack, his movements fluid and controlled. "I will protect my friends, no matter the cost," he replied, his voice steady. The two clashed, their fight a whirlwind of steel and magic. Gabriel's strength and agility allowed him to match Alaric's relentless attacks, but he knew he had to find a way to end the fight quickly.

While Gabriel and Alaric dueled, the rest of the coven played their critical roles. Seraphina unleashed torrents of fire, forcing hunters to retreat. Lyra healed the injured, her gentle touch restoring their strength. Thalia's illusions confused the hunters, making it difficult for them to target the witches accurately.

Cassia and Iris worked together, combining their alchemical knowledge and empathic abilities to create potions that enhanced their powers. Rowan stood as a fierce guardian, her combat skills rivaling those of the hunters.

Each member of the coven contributed to the defense, their unity and cooperation creating a formidable force. They moved with precision, their bond strengthening their resolve. Despite the chaos, there was an undeniable sense of harmony in their actions.

As the battle raged on, a sudden twist changed the course of events. A powerful hunter, cloaked in darkness, appeared on the battlefield. His presence was overwhelming, his aura filled with an ancient and malevolent energy. He was unlike any hunter they had faced before.

Celeste's heart sank as she recognized the figure – it was Malachi, an ancient vampire who had once been a mentor to Gabriel. But now, he stood with the hunters, his eyes filled with betrayal and anger.

"Malachi," Gabriel whispered, his voice filled with disbelief. "Why are you here?"

Malachi's lips curled into a cruel smile. "You have grown weak, Gabriel. You ally yourself with witches and humans, betraying your true nature. I am here to correct that mistake."

The revelation sent shockwaves through the group. The battle took on a new level of intensity as they realized they were not only fighting hunters but also a powerful vampire with a personal vendetta. Celeste and her coven rallied; their determination renewed by the unexpected challenge.

The stage was set for an epic confrontation, the stakes higher than ever. Celeste, Gabriel, and the coven would have to summon all their strength and courage to face Malachi and the hunters. Their bond, their love, and their magic were their only hope against the darkness that threatened to consume them.

Chapter 5
The Final Confrontation

The night air was thick with tension as Celeste, Gabriel, and the coven prepared for the final confrontation. The forest around them was eerily silent, as if the world itself was holding its breath. The scent of pine and damp earth mingled with the metallic tang of anticipation.

Celeste's heart pounded in her chest, her magic swirling around her like a protective cloak. She could feel the power of her coven, each witch a beacon of strength and determination. They stood in a circle, their hands linked, ready to face the darkness together.

Malachi and the hunters emerged from the shadows; their eyes gleaming with malevolent intent. "This ends now," Malachi declared, his voice echoing through the trees. "You cannot escape your fate."

Celeste stepped forward; her voice unwavering. "We make our own fate," she replied. "And we will fight for it."

The battle erupted in a blaze of magic and fury. Spells flew through the air, clashing with the hunters' weapons. The forest was illuminated by bursts of light and fire, the sounds of combat ringing out like a symphony of war.

As the battle raged on, Celeste knew they needed a decisive move to turn the tide. She reached deep within herself, drawing on the ancient magic of her ancestors. With a powerful incantation, she summoned a spell of binding, a weave of light and energy designed to trap Malachi and the hunters.

The ground trembled as the spell took shape, golden tendrils of light snaking towards their enemies. Malachi sensed the danger and countered with his own dark magic, a shadowy force that sought to unravel Celeste's spell.

Celeste's concentration wavered, the strain of the powerful magic taking its toll. Gabriel rushed to her side, lending his strength to bolster her spell. Together, they poured their energy into the incantation, their bond amplifying their power.

With a final, desperate push, the spell snapped into place. The golden tendrils wrapped around Malachi and the hunters, binding them in a cage of light. The forest fell silent, the battle momentarily halted.

Malachi struggled against the binding, his eyes blazing with fury. "You think you can hold me?" he spat. "You are fools."

Gabriel stepped forward; his expression resolute. "This is your last chance, Malachi. Surrender, or face the consequences."

Malachi's laughter was dark and hollow. "You are weak, Gabriel. You always have been. I will never surrender to the likes of you."

Gabriel's heart ached at the betrayal of his former mentor, but he knew what had to be done. He turned to Celeste; his eyes filled with determination. "We have to finish this."

Celeste nodded, understanding the weight of his decision. Together, they channeled their remaining power into the binding spell, strengthening it until it shimmered with an unbreakable force.

The hunters, seeing their leader trapped, began to falter. Some attempted to flee, but the coven was relentless. Seraphina's fire magic blazed through the night, cutting off their escape routes, while Nyx's summoned spirits blocked their paths.

One by one, the hunters were subdued, their weapons falling from their hands as they realized their defeat. The coven's unity and strength had turned the tide, and the threat of the hunters was finally quelled.

But the battle had taken its toll. The witches were exhausted, their magic nearly depleted. Gabriel, too, was drained, his vampiric abilities pushed to their limits. They stood together, a testament to their resilience and determination.

As the dust settled, Celeste approached Malachi, who was still bound by the spell. "Why did you turn against us?" she demanded. "What drove you to this?"

Malachi's eyes were filled with a mixture of anger and regret. "You do not understand the darkness that lies within us, Celeste. The power we wield... it corrupts. I wanted to save Gabriel from that fate, but he chose you instead."

Celeste felt a pang of sympathy but remained resolute. "We all have darkness within us, Malachi. But it is our choices that define us."

Before Malachi could respond, a sudden ripple of magic coursed through the air. Celeste's vision blurred, and she felt a strange sensation, as if the very fabric of reality was shifting.

When her vision cleared, she saw a figure standing at the edge of the clearing. It was a woman, her presence ethereal and powerful. She radiated an ancient magic, her eyes glowing with wisdom and authority.

"Who are you?" Celeste asked, her voice trembling.

The woman smiled, a knowing look in her eyes. "I am Morgana, the guardian of time. You have altered the past, but the future remains uncertain."

Celeste's heart raced. "What does that mean?"

Morgana's smile faded. "It means your journey is far from over. The true test lies ahead, and the fate of both witches and vampires hangs in the balance."

The revelation left Celeste and her companions in stunned silence. They had won the battle, but the war was far from over. Their love, their magic, and their courage would be tested in ways they had never imagined.

As Morgana's words echoed in her mind, Celeste knew they had to be prepared for whatever came next. The stakes were higher than ever, and the future was a shadowy, uncertain path.

Epilogue

The moon hung high in the night sky, casting a silvery glow over the tranquil forest. Celeste stood at the edge of the clearing, the cool breeze whispering through the trees, carrying with it the scent of pine and earth. The battle was over, but the war had only just begun.

Beside her, Gabriel gazed into the distance, his piercing blue eyes filled with a mixture of resolve and uncertainty. The presence of Morgana, the guardian of time, had changed everything. Her words echoed in Celeste's mind, a constant reminder of the challenges that lay ahead.

"You have altered the past, but the future remains uncertain."

The Witch's Prophecy

Celeste knew that their journey was far from over. The balance between light and darkness was delicate, and their actions would determine the fate of both witches and vampires. The path ahead was shrouded in mystery, but she felt a renewed sense of purpose. With Gabriel by her side, she was ready to face whatever trials awaited them.

"We'll get through this," Gabriel said softly, his hand finding hers. "Together."

Celeste nodded, a fire igniting within her. "Together."

As the first light of dawn began to creep over the horizon, Celeste and Gabriel turned away from the clearing, ready to face the future. Their love and determination would be their guiding light in the dark times ahead.

The Witch's Prophecy

Zarua D. Maning

The journey continues in "The Witch's Legacy," coming Winter.

The Witch's Prophecy

Zarua D. Maning

The Witch's Prophecy